BLAZERS

SECRET SERVICE AGENTS

BY ABBY COLICH

CAPSTONE PRESS

Blazers Books are published by Capstone Press,
1710 Roe Crest Drive, North Mankato, Minnesota 56003
www.mycapstone.com

Library of Congress Cataloging-in-Publication Data
Names: Colich, Abby, author.
Title: Secret service agents / by Abby Colich.
Description: North Mankato, Minnesota : Capstone Press, [2018] |
Series: Blazers. U.S. federal agents | Includes bibliographical references and index.
Identifiers: LCCN 2017039232 (print) | LCCN 2017047501 (ebook) |
ISBN 9781543501476 (eBook PDF) | ISBN 9781543501438 (hardcover)
Subjects: LCSH: United States. Secret Service—Juvenile literature. |
Secret service—United States—Juvenile literature.
Classification: LCC HV8144.S43 (ebook) | LCC HV8144.S43 C65 2018 (print) |
DDC 363.28/30973—dc23
LC record available at https://lccn.loc.gov/2017039232

Editorial Credits
Nikki Bruno Clapper, editor; Kyle Grenz, designer; Svetlana Zhurkin, media researcher; Katy LaVigne, production specialist

Photo Credits
Getty Images: AFP/Saul Loeb, 21, AFP/Timothy A. Clary, 20, Bloomberg/Andrew Harrer, 12, The Denver Post/Kathryn Scott Osler, 19; iStockphoto: 1001slide, 11, 400tmax, 10; Library of Congress, 6; Newscom: Reuters/Jonathan Ernst, 5, Reuters/Yuri Gripas, 27, Zuma Press/Stephen Shaver, 28–29; Shutterstock: Andrey_Popov, cover (front), betto rodrigues, 22, cheapbooks, 25, nisargmediaproductions, 8–9, Roman Babakin, 15, Roman Tiraspolsky, 14, Surgeon, cover (top back), wavebreakmedia, 17

Design Elements by Shutterstock

Printed and bound in the USA.
010757S18

Table of Contents

The Secret Service

You follow the president everywhere. You go to the restroom with him. You make sure his food is safe to eat. You are a Secret Service officer. It is your job to protect the president of the United States.

Secret Service officers walk with President Donald Trump.

ITALIA
FLOATER
D
SUMMIT

The Secret Service began in 1865. It stopped people from making fake money. In 1901 someone shot and killed President William McKinley. Soon the Secret Service began to protect the U.S. president.

Just PART of the Job

William McKinley was the third U.S. president to be killed.

A man shoots President William McKinley with a hidden gun.

The Secret Service will always protect former First Lady Michelle Obama.

Just PART of the Job

The Secret Service gives code names to the people it protects.

Today the Secret Service protects the president, the vice president, and their families. They also protect people running for president and **former** presidents and their families.

former—having once been someone or something

Secret Service officers guard **government** buildings. They watch over the White House. They keep people at large events safe. Someone might have a gun or a bomb. Officers look for any danger.

government—the group of people who make laws, rules, and decisions for a country or state

Just PART of the Job

The Secret Service helped keep people safe at the 2016 Super Bowl.

A Secret Service officer guards the White House.

THE UNITED STATES OF AMERICA
IN GOD WE TRUST
100

The Secret Service also solves crimes involving money. The crime could be credit card or bank **fraud**. Special agents also work to stop **identity theft**.

fraud—the practice of cheating or tricking

identity theft—the illegal practice of using information from a person or business for financial gain

SECRET
SERVICE

Just PART of the Job

Countersnipers (below) are uniformed officers. They work on top of buildings. They look for danger below.

Secret Service workers have different jobs. Special agents solve crimes. Special officers protect people and keep equipment running well. Uniformed officers guard buildings and keep events safe.

countersniper—an officer trained to shoot faraway threats from a hidden place

Joining the Secret Service

Getting a job with the Secret Service is not easy. Those who want a job must pass a **background check**. They have to take a **polygraph** test. They must pass a written test too.

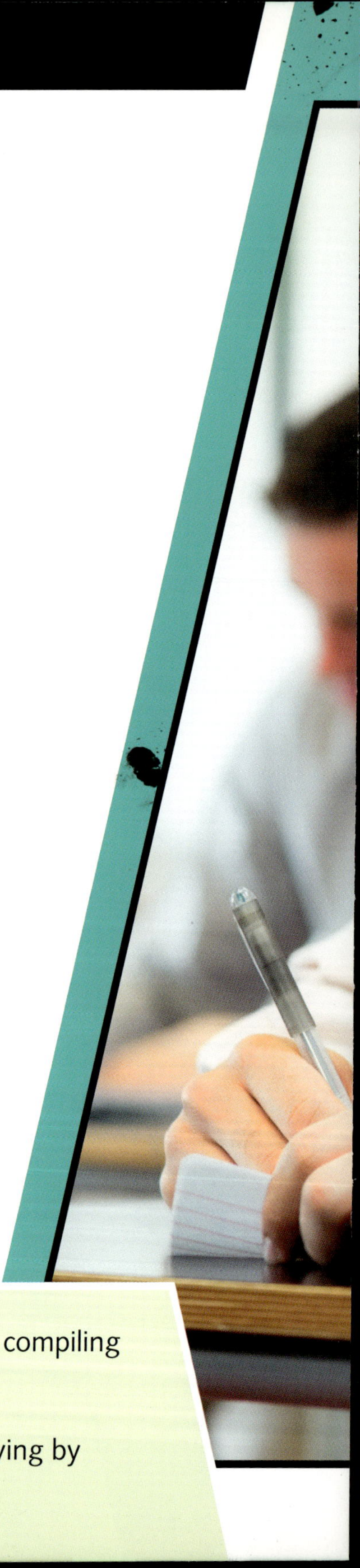

background check—the process of looking up and compiling information about a person

polygraph—a device used to detect if a person is lying by tracking changes in body functions

Training takes months. New officers learn about the law and **policing**. They go through tough physical training. They learn how to use weapons.

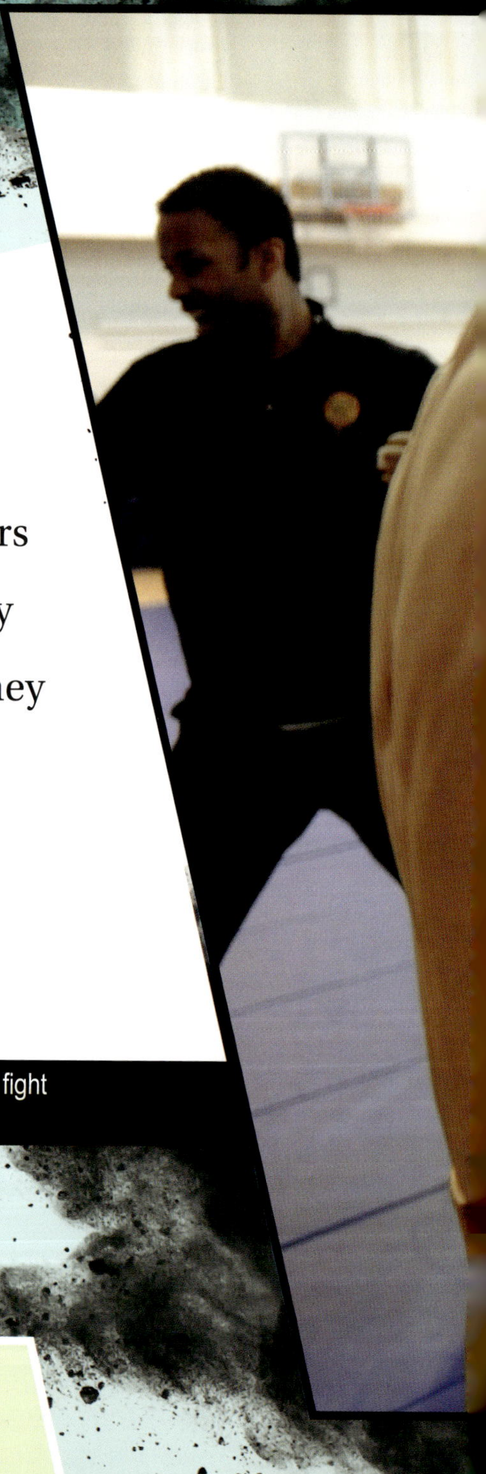

Secret Service officers must learn how to fight hand to hand.

policing—controlling or keeping in order; performing the duties of the police

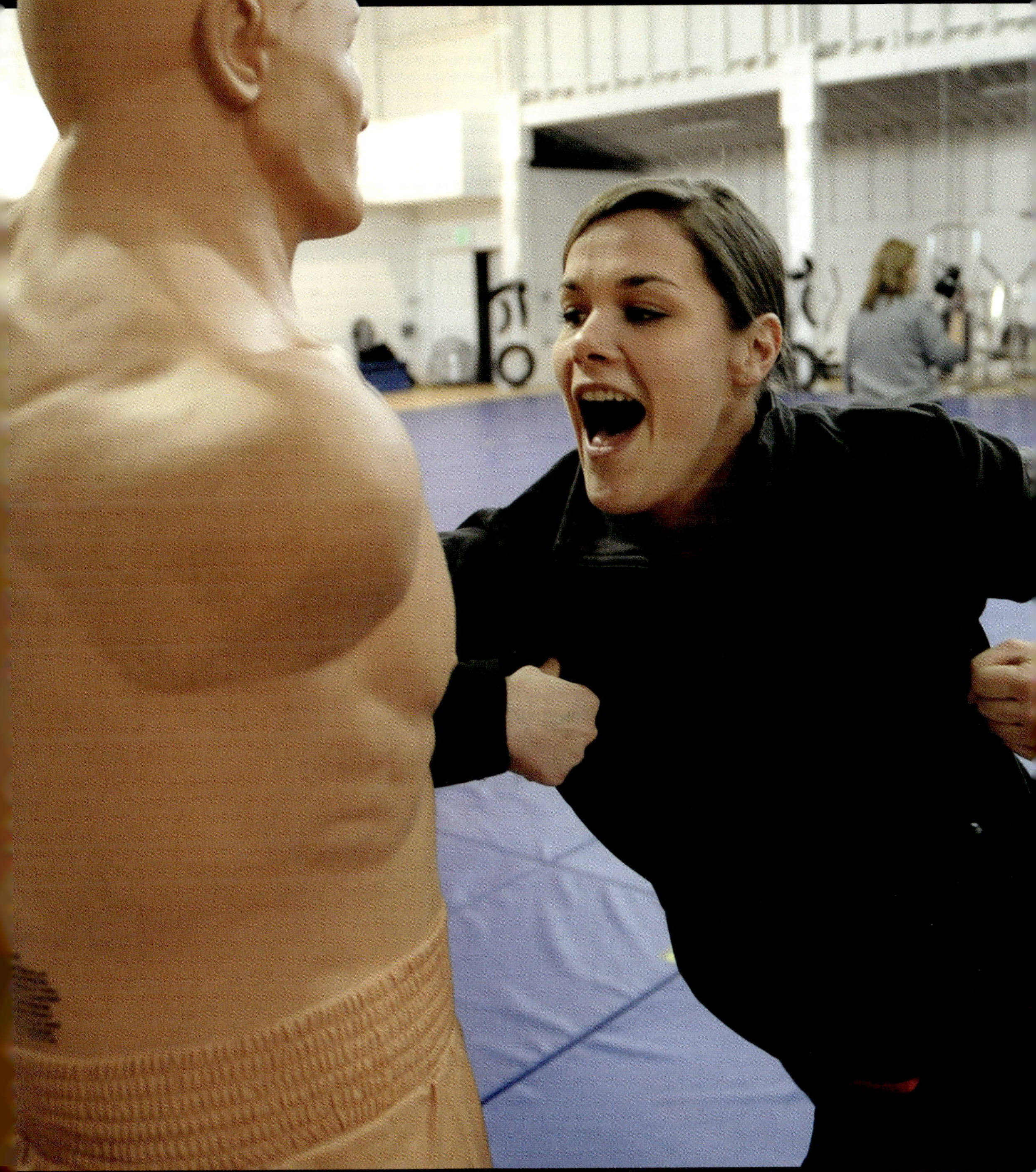

Protecting the President

The Secret Service keeps the president safe at all times. Officers stay near him. Shift agents travel with him. They look for danger. Large crowds are the least safe. It's easy for an attacker to hide.

Just PART of the Job

Officers do not go in the president's office. They stand just outside the door. Weight **sensors** show them where he is.

sensor—a tool that detects changes and sends information to a controlling device

Just PART of the Job

The Secret Service films the president's **motorcade**. Officers watch it later to look for threats or to find attackers.

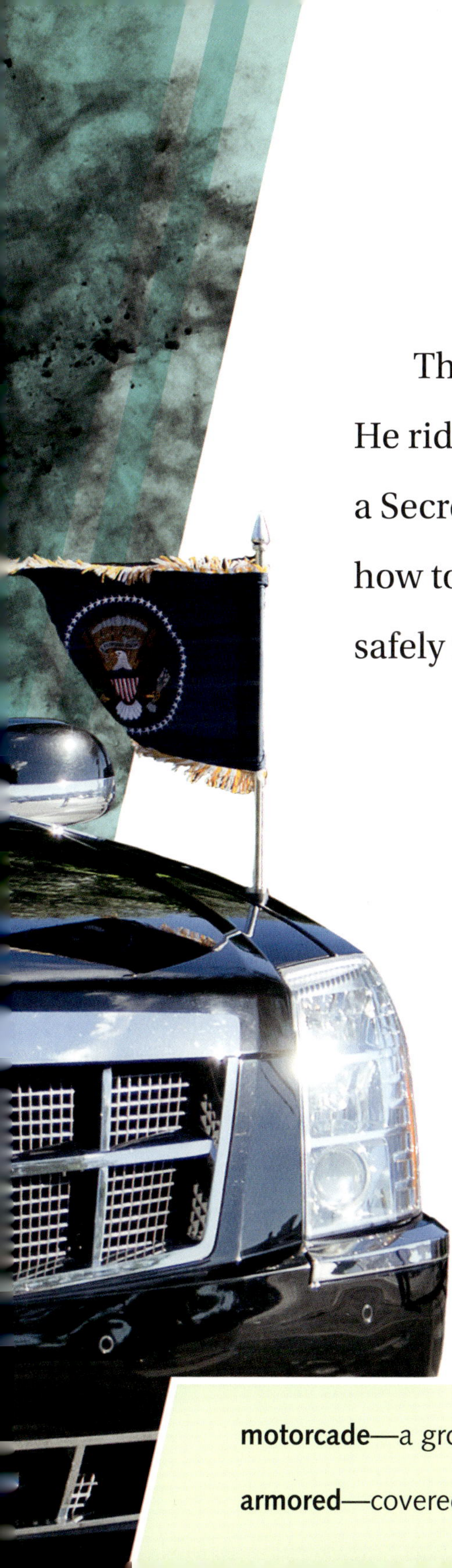

The president travels in a motorcade. He rides in an **armored** car. The driver is a Secret Service officer. The officer knows how to escape danger. He or she can safely make fast, sharp turns.

motorcade—a group of vehicles traveling together

armored—covered with metal to protect against attacks

Most Secret Service officers don't have uniforms. They wear whatever helps them fit in. It's usually a suit. They wear a tiny earpiece. A tiny microphone hides in their sleeve. These tools let officers talk to each other.

Just PART of the Job

Some officers wear disguises. At times they hide under fake grass tarps.

Keeping Events Safe

Site agents help protect people at events. They may plan for months. There could be a medical emergency. There could be a bomb threat. Agents have a plan for anything that can go wrong.

Just PART of the Job

What if the president wants to change plans? It's no problem. A Secret Service "jump team" is ready.

This Secret Service team uses a robot to check for bombs.

Just PART of the Job

Once the president is inside a building, there is a freeze. This means no one can come in or go out.

Agents do a "sweep" of an event site. They check all the buildings. They look for any danger. They use bomb-sniffing dogs. Bulletproof glass covers some of the windows.

Glossary

armored (AR-muhrd)—covered with metal to protect against attacks

background check (BAK-graund CHEK)—the process of looking up and compiling information about a person

countersniper (KAUN-tuhr-sny-pur)—an officer trained to shoot faraway threats from a hidden place

former (FOR-muhr)—having once been someone or something

fraud (FRAWD)—the practice of cheating or tricking

government (GUH-vurn-muhnt)—the group of people who make laws, rules, and decisions for a country or state

identity theft (eye-DEN-ti-tee THEFT)—the illegal practice of using information from a person or business for financial gain

motorcade (MOH-turh-kade)—a group of vehicles traveling together

policing (puh-LEESS-ing)—controlling or keeping in order; performing the duties of the police

polygraph (PAWL-ee-graf)—a device used to detect if a person is lying by tracking changes in body functions

sensor (SEN-sur)—a tool that detects changes and sends information to a controlling device

Read More

Cane, Ella. *The U.S. Presidency.* Our Government. North Mankato, Minn.: Capstone, 2014.

Shea, Therese. *A Career as a Secret Service Agent.* Federal Forces: Careers as Federal Agents. New York: PowerKids Press, 2016.

Waters, Kate. *Curious about the White House.* New York: Grosset and Dunlap, an imprint of Penguin Random House, 2016.

Internet Sites

Use FactHound to find Internet sites related to this book.

Visit *www.facthound.com*

Just type in 9781543501438 and go.

Index